The Ugly Duck Thing

For Isabella Jean Herfet,
with Seriously Silly wishes
LA

For

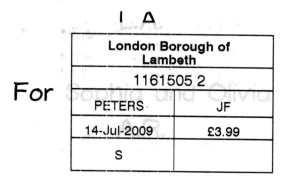

London Borough of Lambeth	
1161505 2	
PETERS	JF
14-Jul-2009	£3.99
S	

Visit Laurence Anholt's website at
www.anholt.co.uk

ORCHARD BOOKS
338 Euston Road
London NW3 3BH
Orchard Books Australia
Level 17-207 Kent Street, Sydney, NSW 2000, Australia

First published by Orchard Books in 2008
First paperback publication in 2009

Text © Laurence Anholt 2008
Illustrations © Arthur Robins 2008

The rights of Laurence Anholt to be identified as the author
and of Arthur Robins to be identified as the illustrator
of this work have been asserted by them in accordance
with the Copyright, Designs and Patents Act, 1988.

A CIP catalogue record for this book is available from the British Library.

ISBN 978 1 84616 076 9 (hardback)
ISBN 978 1 84616 314 2 (paperback)

1 2 3 4 5 6 7 8 9 10 (hardback)
1 2 3 4 5 6 7 8 9 10 (paperback)

Printed in China

Orchard Books is a division of Hachette Children's Books,
an Hachette Livre UK company.
www.hachettelivre.co.uk

Laurence Anholt   Arthur Robins

seriously SILLY colour

Duck!

The Ugly Duck Thing

ORCHARD BOOKS

In a wooden shack lived
a Mummy Duck.

Mummy Duck laid six brown eggs.

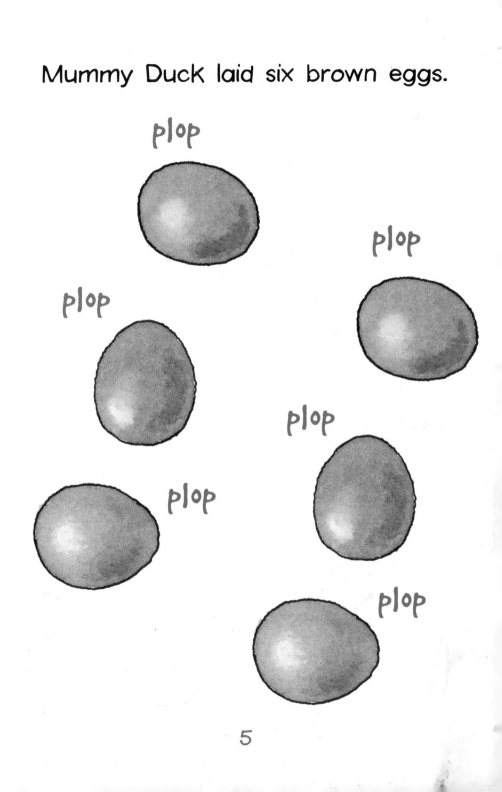

She was very proud.

But one morning,
a bee flew into
the shack.

Quack, quack!
I'm under
attack!

And one lovely egg rolled
off the stack and out of
the back of the shack.

7

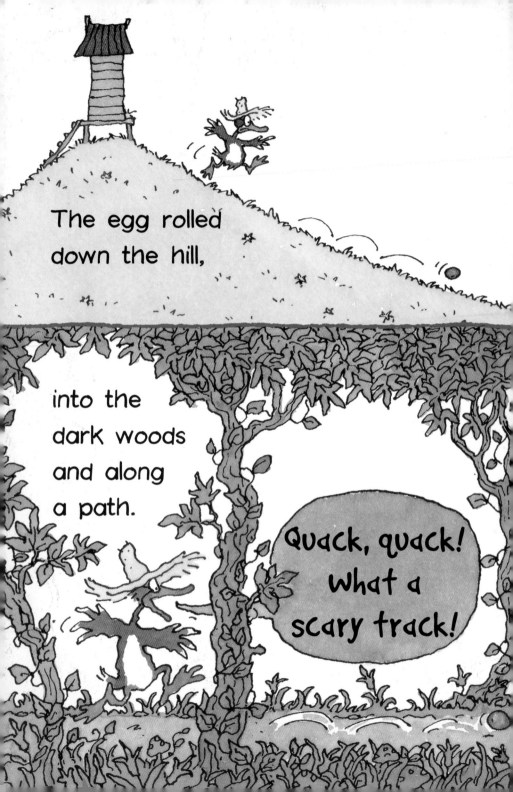

At last, Mummy Duck's egg
tumbled into a huge cave.

Quack, quack!
Everything's black!

Mummy Duck fumbled in the dark
and found an egg.

She put the
egg carefully
in her nest
and sat down
to wait.

Then she heard
a little noise.

Quack, quack!
They're starting
to crack!

Crack!

Crack!

Out popped five
tiny, fluffy ducklings.

13

And **Crack!**
Out popped one
enormous Ugly
Duck Thing.

Quack, quack!
He's as big
as a yak!

The Ugly Duck Thing
was so big that he
hit his head on the
roof of the shack.

Quack quack!
What a whack!

So Mummy Duck put
a sign above
the door:

The little ducklings grew
a tiny bit every day.
But the Ugly Duck Thing
grew huge and HUNGRY!

The Ugly Duck Thing did not
want a tiny worm for tea, he
wanted something much bigger.

Quack, quack!
A whole haystack!

18

Mummy Duck taught the
five ducklings to swim.

Quack, quack!
You'll soon
get the knack

The Ugly Duck Thing grew
too big to live in the shack.
He decided to go into the world.

He walked a long way. Wherever he went people laughed at him.

Look at that Ugly Duck Thing

The Ugly Duck Thing felt very sad

He found a job cutting down trees and wrote a letter to Mummy Duck.

Quack, quack! He's a lumberjack

But the Ugly Duck Thing ate too many trees and lost his job.

The Ugly Duck Thing walked some more and got very lost.

He came to a dark wood
and found a nice cave.

In the cave was . . .

. . . a whole family of
big Ugly Duck Things!
They were just like him.
The Ugly Duck Thing
was very happy.

In the corner of the cave was one tiny Duck Thing.

He won't eat anything except worms. He never seems to grow

The Ugly Duck Thing looked at the tiny Duck Thing.

I think I know where you belong

He carried him on his back up
the track to the shack.

Mummy Duck was very pleased
to see the Ugly Duck Thing.
And she was even more pleased
to see her own baby duckling.

The Ugly Duck Thing went to live
with his real family in the cave.

They said he was the most beautiful Duck Thing they had ever seen and made him their king.

Laurence Anholt Arthur Robins

seriously SILLY colour

ENJOY ALL THESE SERIOUSLY SILLY STORIES!

All priced at £3.99

Orchard books are available from all good bookshops, or can be ordered direct from the publisher:
Orchard Books, PO BOX 29, Douglas IM99 1BQ
Credit card orders please telephone: 01624 836000 or fax: 01624 837033
or visit our website: www.orchardbooks.co.uk or e-mail: bookshop@enterprise.net for details.

To order please quote title, author and ISBN and your full name and address.
Cheques and postal orders should be made payable to 'Bookpost plc.'
Postage and packing is FREE within the UK (overseas customers should add £1.00 per book).

Prices and availability are subject to change.